Awakenings

The Life Erotic: Part One
A Discovery Journal

By Athena, writing as B. Unbidden

Second Edition Print 2023
ISBN: 978-1-960298-00-3 (print)
ISBN: 978-1-960298-02-7 (EPUB)

Published by Elder Glade Publishing, LLC
www.eldergladepublishing.com

Dedication

*How fierce and sudden my heat
rises for you, Lover.*

*I, Blush Unbidden, bloom for
your touch.*

For you.

Monday:
Twixt the Two

I woke in the 'tween time—not yesterday, nor yet tomorrow, but the sliver of clock twixt the two—and gazed upon the night pose of my lover, twined through my limbs. The moonlit hollow of your throat, where beat the rhythm of my greatest adoration, drew my attention. I shifted, so as not to wake you, and pressed my lips to your pulse. Your warm skin and tangy sweat against the tip of my tongue tasted of musical pheromones and the sex we'd spent ourselves upon not hours before.

I delighted so much in the flavor that my breath quickened. A warm glow suffused my already exhausted thighs, and I knew I must have you again. Yes, again.

Gently, to bring you to me in dreamy longings, as we'd already agreed upon as your preferred style of being wakened, I slipped a hand down your belly. You moaned in your sleep, shifting slightly. I waited for you to settle, then feathered my fingers around your balls and stroked until you stirred … hungry.

Tuesday: Under the Table

We laughed, chatting comfortably during dinner on the roof of the restaurant overlooking the city. As dessert was served, and the server disappeared for another bottle of wine, you slid beneath the table, hidden by the tablecloth. Then you shimmied my dress up around my hips and spread my legs. I wasn't wearing panties, and you slipped by my garter straps. As you helped yourself to my tender lips, my swollen clit and juices, the server returned. I struggled to remain composed and answer his questions as you drove me to distraction—sweet, merciless torture.

Did we enjoy our meal? "Yes. Very much," I assured him with a shiver.

Was I enjoying the visit to the city? I nodded and whimpered, "Yes. Yes, I am."

Would I care for a box to take home the leftovers? "God, yes!"

The server startled at my enthusiasm. I quickly added, "Thank you," with a sigh, then fell silent, bit my lip, and focused to keep from moaning or bucking the table. The poor fellow.

As I went still, you took the opportunity to slip a finger deep inside my body. I jumped and sighed, shuddering before the bewildered young man. My face burned, cheeks aflame; my juices ran hotter still. When he left, I passed a glass of merlot to you under the tablecloth, then leaned back against the seat, admiring the city as you mixed wine, dessert, and my pussy on your tongue.

In the limousine, headed back to the hotel, I pushed you against the leather, repaying the favor as the city lights passed by.

Wednesday: Peaches

I don't cook often, so I was unduly pleased with myself that the scallops were sautéing beautifully with the peaches when you walked in. I saw your expression and knew the day you'd had.

"Darling," I said as I poured you a glass of wine. "Wanna talk about it?"

You took the glass and kissed me. As your scruff rubbed my chin, my body lit up. I smiled against you. "I'm glad you're home."

You rested the glass on the counter, wrapped your arms around my body, pulling me tight, and kissed me deeply, hungrily, thoroughly. I melted into your embrace, clutching at your arms to keep steady.

You were quick, backing me up against the marble surface. Then you spun me around, bent me over the counter, lifted my dress, and gripped my cheeks. You growled and leaned over to nibble.

"My day is suddenly much better," you mumbled between mouthfuls.

I laughed and you chuckled before grinding against me. You were hard and hungry, and I was extra pleased with myself that I'd tried cooking, since it had clearly worked so well in my favor. Then, as my giggles turned to breathlessness, and my hips bucked against you, you slipped my panties aside, gracing me your fingers.

I gasped, moaned, and collapsed against the counter, presenting my ass to you, however you'd care to take me. Just please, for the love of god, take me now!

Always the gentleman, you obliged my request.

I heard your zipper, felt the pressure of your cock. I held my breath, my thighs quivering with the struggle to stay upright, to wait for it. When you sank into my body I grabbed at the counter, clutching at anything that might keep me from flying apart, arms flailing wildly for purchase. The pepper mill crashed to the floor as you plugged me deeply and rode me thoroughly, my knees knocking against the cabinets.

As you gripped my hips, thrusting, and I whimpered, moaning, you pulled my head back and tongued me hard, your fingers cupping my throat. I tangled one arm through yours to keep my balance while you kissed me as if had been days since you'd last eaten—though I knew full well you'd had me for breakfast, too.

I came, ruining your beautiful suit, again. I languished for a moment in the post-orgasm glow before I smelled something burning.

"Shit!" you shouted, and suddenly pulled out.

I wobbled, and grabbed the sink to keep from falling as you quickly turned off the stove flame and slid the pan of burnt scallops and peaches to a different burner.

"Damn," I grumbled. "Didn't that happen the last time I tried to make this recipe?"

You grinned and turned around, wet cock standing out of your pants. "It must be something about your peaches, Baby."

I laughed. "I'll show you my peaches … come here." I grabbed your tie, dragging you closer. Kneeling on the kitchen rug, I took your cock in my hands.

You were still smiling when I slipped you in my mouth and cupped your balls, stopping your teasing. You sighed, seizing the counter with one hand, my hair with the other.

Dinner was ruined, but at least dessert had been saved.

Thursday: Magic

You clutched my thighs, indent-ing pale flesh as you held me firm. I knew you meant to torture me by the seriousness of your grip. Then, casually, as though tomorrow were a thousand years away, you licked my pussy—long, massaging strokes with a warm tongue. You kneaded my lips with your own, suckling, pulling, kissing—driving me to passionate begging and breathless promises. I bargained, bucked, and squirmed to no avail. I wriggled, pled, and tangled my fingers in your dark hair. I threatened, conferred, and then fell silent with the pleasurable agony of frustration.

You held me firmly from the edge of climax, teetering but never allowed to fly. Then you clutched my ass cheeks, near to bruising, held your mouth just eyelashes from my soaked lady bits ... and froze.

The room smelled of sex, a rich, lusty tonic laced with a hint of unexplored depths. The hazy scent of something darker, deeper to be tasted ... when the time was right.

"Baby, please," I whimpered, piqued by my own desperation. "I want you in me."

Still, you paused, waiting for the

quiver in my thighs to turn to shaking, then aching stillness. The moment my body relaxed your tongue flicked out, wetting my clit, and you whispered against my swollen flesh. "I want your juices, Sweetness." Then you slipped two fingers inside me.

My ragged gasp of release, the hot squirt of passion followed by panting, near-animal sounds of need, as I rode your face and fingers, made you stiffen. You were sturdy, hard, and wanting, yet you drove me through the orgasm wildlands again, then yet again. Your unbreakable hold on my body, as I writhed, turned from cupping my flesh to banding your long, muscular arms around my hips. You used my body against me as I spasmed, flexed, and shouted your name in both praise and admonition, cursing and begging as I thanked you with one long surrender after another.

My legs trembled, then relaxed. Tears of release left mascara tracks on my cheeks, and my saucy cum soaked the sheets. I was properly spent—muscles puddled to tenderized perfection.

You stood, wiped a meaty hand across your wet, wicked grin, and said, "You taste like magic."

Then you grabbed my legs, my weak, wobbly legs, dragged me toward your naked, glorious body, and said, "I bet you feel like magic, too."

Friday: Haven

Rain pelted the windows, a lullaby soothing my heart from a long week of worldly disappointments: unhappy editors, disagreeable readers, frustrated designers, and so on. It seemed I could please no one.

You sat on the sofa near the lamp, poring through work documents with a glass of amber liquid in one hand. You scrubbed your chin and ran a hand through your dark hair. I realized we were of the same congested mind. I set my manuscript aside; editing could wait.

I shuffled by you in my panties and tank top. That I barely drew your notice from the stack of papers let me know how badly off you really were. I sidled behind you and casually ran my fingers along your shoulder, then gently massaged your neck.

You sighed and leaned your head back into my touch. "I can't believe they missed these reports in the quality department."

I smiled and kissed your forehead, agreeing softly. "I know, Baby."

After a few moments of my caresses, you opened your eyes and said, almost painfully, "I really want you right now, but I have to finish this tonight."

I nuzzled your cheek. "May I keep you company?"

You nodded as I kissed you. Then I wandered around to the front of the sofa, where you adjusted to make space. I sat on your lap, noting your rigid length beneath my hip, then I leaned against your chest, curled up, and relaxed. You placed your Scotch on the end table and wrapped an arm around my body.

I rested peacefully in your embrace as you puzzled through work issues. The tension fled your muscles, draining into stillness. Your breathing slowed. The stiffness in your shoulders eased. At length I fell asleep, snug against you.

Sometime in the night, as the rain dwindled and the clock swiveled days, you shifted. I stirred.

"Shh," you whispered. "I've got you." You carried me to bed, where we sank into the blankets, worn down by the week but having found haven in one another. Our loving was quick and tired, but in the midnight hours, when you tucked yourself inside my body and I wrapped myself around you, I smiled, contented, half asleep, half in a dream, not caring for anything but that you filled me.

Saturday: One Day at a Time

We drove to the coast for the day, a short, winding trip through the hills to the sea. Winter storms tormented the small town where we stopped for lunch; clam chowder and a view.

Rain slammed the streets, the sand. The ocean boiled in tempest. There was nothing gentle or sweet about the torrent of Mother Nature. Thunder and lightning and the roar of angry surf were our Saturday lunch serenade. We warmed our hands and bellies with soup, chatting lightly about our plans for the upcoming week.

We were both locked into deadlines and more deadlines, with no end in sight. Still, we hoped the spring would bring a chance for a small romantic getaway. We craved time to be truly alone and explore one another in depth, yet we couldn't agree on timing, our schedules a hopeless labyrinth.

It was on the drive home, along the highway through the old-growth forests, that I gazed out the window at the trees gowned in moss, with carpets of fern dressing the paths. The rain continued to pound; the wipers beat on the highest setting.

I worried we'd never find the time

to escape with one another, that our adventures would be just moments in the week. We'd be relegated to a quick trip to the coastline, then back to the grind. I watched the forest and wondered when I'd be able to relax into you. Really lean in and take three full, deep breaths of you, pull you into my body and not worry that I might be asking too high or wanting beyond what you could offer.

A fission of old fear bloomed, deep and terrifying, within. An old angst of wanting too much, of being denied, of crushing someone with my desires, took shape into the familiar pattern of withdrawal. I sighed and rested my head against the window.

You glanced over. "Talk to me, Beautiful. I know that look."

I knew that tone of voice, too. You only used that tone, the coaxing velvet center surrounded by *I'll get the truth out of you even if I have to wrap your thighs around my face for three hours* tone of voice. You only used it when you knew I was withholding something—sometimes the whole truth, sometimes orgasm, but they were usually the same.

My skin flushed at the thought of you milking the truth from me, but the fear remained.

I whispered, "I'm worried we're never going to get away together—to, you know … go deeper … reach into all the fantasies we've talked about."

I felt your frown more than saw it, and knew you were unhappy with my doubt. You pulled the car off the highway, onto a muddy logging road in the forest. Your silence worried me more than it should have.

When we were out of view from the highway, surrounded by the trees, you stopped the car and got out. My stomach dropped. Was I wrong to have said what was on my mind, voice my genuine concern, before I pulled in tight and closed back up?

You walked around to the passenger side and opened the door. In just a few moments you'd been soaked. You stripped off your jacket, standing in the rain in your T-shirt and jeans, then held a hand out in invitation.

"My Lady," you said, meeting my eyes.

You smiled, but I was confused.

"You spoke of fantasies, right? Of the things you want to try. The depth?" You leaned in, dripping on my lap. "If we only get a moment at a time, let's go as deep as we can in each of those moments." Your eyes gleamed, shining with invitation.

You held your hand out again; this time I took it.

You pulled me up into the rain, the cold winter rain of the Pacific North-west. Frigid and unkind. But you drew me against your body, slid my jacket off my shoulders and tossed it in the car. We were quickly drenched, chilled. Yet, to my amazement, I was utterly lit up by your surety.

"You wanted to dance the tango when we had time to learn it," you said.

I nodded against your chest and looked up.

"What if this is the only chance we ever get?" You kissed me, then gripped my body, one hand in mine, the other on my lower back, and whispered, "If I only get to have you one bite at a time, one little nibble here and there—I'll take it, say thank you, and be hungry for more, but I'll never pull away because of that hunger, ever."

I shook in your grip, but not from the cold.

Then you led me in a dance. I didn't follow; I joined. I wasn't dragged; I stepped gratefully. I didn't tuck in or pull back; I gave what I had and hoped it would be enough for both of us, until we could have each other uninterrupted between the rush of trying to live—that we could, in this moment, be alive.

The logging road was muddy. We slipped and slid as we splashed and danced. It wasn't the sexy tango of my imagination—it was more. It was raw, a little desperate, with a childlike wonder mixed with the pleasure of just being free. Before I could help myself, I was laughing.

Then we were kissing and fumbling with each other's wet clothes. We staggered against the car as I peeled your soggy shirt over your head. You shuffled my jeans down my hips.

You were hard. I couldn't wait to get my hands on you, but you were faster, and my fingers wouldn't bend for the cold. With my jeans puddled around my ankles, your chilled hands splayed me open for the taking. I gasped.

I'd brought out your fear by acknowledging my own, and your animal response was as much a claiming as a need to remind me you were flesh and man and so much human that I couldn't possibly forget you needed me, too. What a pair we made.

You thrust into me, hard, gripping the back of my neck, crushing me against your body and the car as you drove balls deep, hungry deep, fearful deep—hopeful deep. Filling my cold body with your heat.

With each stroke you said in my ear, "As deep as we can go. One day at a time."

I came in a torrent of warm fluid. You followed shortly after, then caught us both as I sagged, panting. You wrapped an arm around my waist and buried your face in my wet neck. You kissed me tenderly and said, "We're okay. We're going to be fine."

I nodded, then sighed as you pulled out. Hot cum trickled down my pale thighs. You swiped a hand up my leg, then kissed my forehead gently.

You quickly wrapped me in a blanket from the trunk. The drive back to town was quiet, your fingers laced in mine. Each time I found myself smiling, I glanced over to see you grinning, too.

One day at a time, then. I can do that.

Sunday Worship: Reawakening

Dearest Beloved,

I'm writing to you in my discovery journal, again. Still, I struggle to find words when I look at you, when our bodies braid together and the world seems perfectly aligned. My tongue forgets language and I can only speak with my hips, fingers, and eyes. Then we're spent and we fall into one another, and all the words I wish I'd uttered come to mind as you slumber, exhausted, in my embrace. I cannot wake you, dare not for love, dare not for fear of revealing my true depths.

My hips sang what my heart can barely contain—that I adore you beyond reason.

Sunday worship is spent at my writing room window, reliving a week of the unfettered pleasures of your touch. My daily enjoyment of you is a beautiful luxury that has become vitality, a need … a perpetually unquenchable thirst.

How did that happen? When? The realization struck me this week as my lips passed over the scruff of your jaw and your arms flexed around me. Your breath was hot in my ear as you whispered, "I'll go get the car. Wait here by the light, where it's dry." You kissed my cheek and stepped off the curb toward the dark parking garage across the street.

It was that simple. That very moment, as the cold air swept in to replace your touch, and the chill fringed my thigh where your hand had rested on my leg throughout dinner—it was that moment I knew the true absence of you would one day break me.

I tugged my dress, smoothed out the edges and glanced around, certain someone would have noticed the sudden, vulnerable shake in my knees, the sharp intake of breath. For the first time in what felt like a hundred years of a fairytale enchanted slumber ... something inside me was waking.

It woke slowly each time you

smiled, or the graveled thunder of your morning purr against my nether lips brought me to easy climax, followed by your teasing chuckle. It woke in me each time you nuzzled my temple with your nose, cupping my fingers in yours, and said my name in a tone somewhere between wonder and pain. It woke in me when you laughed, and helped me with simple tasks I could have easily done myself, but you asked, gently, if you could do something anyway. It woke each time I rode your body, your muscles sliding under my weight and your breath shifted from focus to fractured containment to primal gasps—and I woke a little each time you filled me, spilling into me your promises. Promises I have begun to believe, to rely upon. The richness of those promises makes me wet, my nipples tight.

I never thought I'd believe again. And yet … as you walked toward the parking garage, you let out an adorable whistle and turned back with a cheeky grin before disappearing into the darkness. I held my breath, panic rising. An insecurity I hadn't known in ages bubbled up, and for a moment I worried you'd left me on the corner for good. You wouldn't be the first— probably not the last.

My hands shook. I tucked them into my jacket, pulling the edges tight.

Then, like the sun rising at dawn after the longest night, your car turned the bottom curve of the garage and pulled out onto the street. You drove up to the curb, got out, and walked around. The tension left my knees and I began to shiver with full force.

"You waited for me?" You teased and kissed my neck. "You should have run off with that flirty bartender while you had the chance."

Your fingers clutched mine and gave a little squeeze. Pain bloomed in my chest as I realized—we'd just tested one another, and ourselves. We're all humans; we've all had heartbreak. None of us have escaped the crosshairs of betrayal, but for tonight, for this evening, we'd met somewhere in the middle of intimacy. In one innocuous moment, we'd caught each other.

"You're freezing. Here, get in."
You pecked my temple, smiled, and
met my eyes. "God, you're beautiful."
Then you opened the door.

My blush rose, unbidden.

As we pulled away from the curb,
I rested my hand on your knee and
glanced over. The city glow lit your
angled chin and dark, deep-set eyes.
Here we go. It's a risk, but Holy Aph-
rodite, what a man, one who is worth
such a risk. He's worth waking up for,
even if it wrecks me.

And I promised to show you my
appreciation of your risk when we
got home. When the candles sput-
tered and the world was still—I'd
tell you with my hips, my fingers, my
eyes, because my tongue has forgot-
ten how to say …

Beloved, believing in you is quite possibly the sexiest fucking thing I've ever experienced.

About the Author

Blush Unbidden is the nom de plume for an author of multiple works under various genres.

To B(e) Unbidden, is the freedom to dance, to live unfettered, enjoying the delicious abundance of love and life without restraint, without shame or judgment or recrimination. Only wild abandon along the sacred sexual journey of give and take, of grace and surrender, of falling deeply and uncontrollably in love with the vulnerability of being human.

Discover more B. Unbidden works at www.ElderGladePublishing.com.

To be continued in...

Nibbles

The Life Erotic: Part Two

A Discovery Journal

By Athena, writing as B. Unbidden

www.ingramcontent.com/pod-product-compliance
Lightning Source LLC
Chambersburg PA
CBHW071254130726
47998CB00003B/1189